"I've got the baby here," Imogene barked at the Wise Men. "Don't touch him! I named him Jesus."

"No, no, no." Mother came flying up the aisle. "Now Imogene, you know you're not supposed to say anything. Nobody says anything in our pageant, except the Angel of the Lord and the choir singing carols. Mary and Joseph and the Wise Men make a lovely picture for us to look at while we think about Christmas and what it means."

"I think I ought to tell them what his name is," Imogene said.

"No. Besides, you remember it wasn't Mary who named the baby."

"I told you!" Ralph whacked Imogene on the back. "I named him."

"Joseph didn't name the baby either," Mother said. "God sent an angel to tell Mary what his name should be."

Imogene sniffed. "I would have named him Bill."

"A refreshingly breezy Christmas book, fast-moving, and very funny."   —*The Horn Book*

"Funny and touching."   —*ALA Booklist*

THE BEST CHRISTMAS PAGEANT EVER

Barbara Robinson

THE BEST CHRISTMAS PAGEANT EVER

Pictures by
Judith Gwyn Brown

HarperTrophy®
A Division of HarperCollinsPublishers

Harper Trophy® is a registered trademark of
HarperCollins Publishers Inc.

A short version of this book appeared in *McCall's Magazine*
under the title "The Christmas Pageant."

The Best Christmas Pageant Ever

Library of Congress Catalog Card Number 72-76501

ISBN 0-06-025043-7
ISBN 0-06-025044-5 (lib. bdg.)
ISBN 0-06-447044-X (pbk.)
First Harper Trophy edition, 1988.

19 20 QGM 50 49 48 47 46 45 44 43

For Jack, of course

THE BEST
CHRISTMAS
PAGEANT
EVER

1

The Herdmans were absolutely the worst kids in the history of the world. They lied and stole and smoked cigars (even the girls) and talked dirty and hit little kids and cussed their teachers and took the name of the Lord in vain and set fire to Fred Shoemaker's old broken-down toolhouse.

The toolhouse burned right down to the ground, and I think that surprised the Herdmans. They set fire to things all the time, but that was the first time they managed to burn down a whole building.

I guess it was an accident. I don't suppose they woke up that morning and said to one another, "Let's go burn down Fred Shoemaker's toolhouse" . . . but maybe they did. After all, it was a Saturday, and not much going on.

1

It was a terrific fire—two engines and two police cars and all the volunteer firemen and five dozen doughnuts sent up from the Tasti-Lunch Diner. The doughnuts were supposed to be for the firemen, but by the time they got the fire out the doughnuts were all gone. The Herdmans got them—what they couldn't eat they stuffed in their pockets and down the front of their shirts. You could actually *see* the doughnuts all around Ollie Herdman's middle.

I couldn't understand why the Herdmans were hanging around the scene of their crime. Everybody knew the whole thing was their fault, and you'd think they'd have the brains to get out of sight.

One fireman even collared Claude Herdman and said, "Did you kids start this fire, smoking cigars in that toolhouse?"

But Claude just said, "We weren't smoking cigars."

And they weren't. They were playing with Leroy Herdman's "Young Einstein" chemistry set, which he stole from the hardware store, and that was how they started the fire.

Leroy said so. "We mixed all the little powders together," he said, "and poured lighter fluid around on them and set fire to the lighter fluid. We wanted to see if the chemistry set was any good."

Any other kid—even a mean kid—would have been a little bit worried if he stole $4.95 worth of something and then burned down a building with it. But Leroy was just mad because the chemistry set got burned up along with everything else before he had a chance to make one or two bombs.

The fire chief got us all together—there were fifteen or twenty kids standing around watching the fire—and gave us a little talk about playing with matches and gasoline and dangerous things like that.

"I don't say that's what happened here," he told us. "I don't *know* what happened here, but that could have been it, and you see the result. So let this be a good lesson to you, boys and girls."

Of course it was a great lesson to the Herdmans —they learned that wherever there's a fire there will be free doughnuts sooner or later.

I guess things would have been different if they'd burned down, say, the Second Presbyterian Church instead of the toolhouse, but the toolhouse was about to fall down anyway. All the neighbors had pestered Mr. Shoemaker to do something about it because it looked so awful and was sure to bring rats. So everybody said the fire was a blessing in disguise, and even Mr. Shoemaker said it was a relief. My father said it was the only good thing the Herdmans ever did, and if they'd *known* it was a good thing, they wouldn't have done it at all. They would have set fire to something else . . . or somebody.

They were just so all-around awful you could hardly believe they were real: Ralph, Imogene, Leroy, Claude, Ollie, and Gladys—six skinny, stringy-haired kids all alike except for being different sizes and having different black-and-blue places where they had clonked each other.

They lived over a garage at the bottom of Sproul Hill. Nobody used the garage anymore, but the Herdmans used to bang the door up and down just as fast as they could and try to squash one another—that was their idea of a game. Where other people had grass in their front yard, the Herdmans had rocks. And where other people had hydrangea bushes, the Herdmans had poison ivy.

There was also a sign in the yard that said "Beware Of The Cat."

New kids always laughed about that till they got a look at the cat. It was the meanest looking animal I ever saw. It had one short leg and a broken tail and one missing eye, and the mailman wouldn't deliver anything to the Herdmans because of it.

"I don't think it's a regular cat at all," the mailman told my father. "I think those kids went up in the hills and caught themselves a bobcat."

"Oh, I don't think you can tame a wild bobcat," my father said.

"I'm sure you can't," said the mailman. "They'd never try to *tame* it; they'd just try to make it wilder than it was to begin with."

4

If that was their plan, it worked—the cat would attack anything it could see out of its one eye.

One day Claude Herdman emptied the whole first grade in three minutes flat when he took the cat to Show-and-Tell. He didn't feed it for two days so it was already mad, and then he carried it to school in a box, and when he opened the box the cat shot out—right straight up in the air, people said.

It came down on the top blackboard ledge and clawed four big long scratches all the way down the blackboard. Then it just tore around all over the place, scratching little kids and shedding fur and scattering books and papers everywhere.

The teacher, Miss Brandel, yelled for everybody to run out in the hall, and she pulled a coat over her head and grabbed a broom and tried to corner the cat. But of course she couldn't see, with the coat over her head, so she just ran up and down the aisles, hollering "Here, kitty!" and smacking the broom down whenever the cat hissed back. She knocked over the Happy Family dollhouse and a globe of the world, and broke the aquarium full of twenty gallons of water and about sixty-five goldfish.

All the time she kept yelling for Claude to come and catch his cat, but Claude had gone out in the hall with the rest of the class.

Later, when Miss Brandel was slapping Band-Aids on everyone who could show her any blood,

she asked Claude why in the world he didn't come and get his cat under control.

"You told us to go out in the hall," Claude said, just as if he were the ordinary kind of first-grader who did whatever teachers said to do.

The cat settled down a little bit once it got something to eat—most of the goldfish and Ramona Billian's two pet mice that she brought to Show-and-Tell. Ramona cried and carried on so—"I can't even bury them!" she said—that they sent her home.

The room was a wreck—broken glass and papers and books and puddles of water and dead goldfish everywhere. Miss Brandel was sort of a wreck too, and most of the first graders were hysterical, so somebody took them outdoors and let them have recess for the rest of the day.

Claude took the cat home and after that there was a rule that you couldn't bring anything alive to Show-and-Tell.

The Herdmans moved from grade to grade through the Woodrow Wilson School like those South American fish that strip your bones clean in three minutes flat . . . which was just about what they did to one teacher after another.

But they never, never got kept back in a grade.

When it came time for Claude Herdman to pass to the second grade he didn't know his ABC's or his numbers or his colors or his shapes or his "Three Bears" or how to get along with anybody.

But Miss Brandel passed him anyway.

For one thing, she knew she'd have Ollie Herdman the next year. That was the thing about the Herdmans—there was always another one coming along, and no teacher was crazy enough to let herself in for two of them at once.

I was always in the same grade with Imogene Herdman, and what I did was stay out of her way. It wasn't easy to stay out of her way. You couldn't do it if you were very pretty or very ugly, or very smart or very dumb, or had anything unusual about you, like red hair or double-jointed thumbs.

But if you were sort of a medium kid like me, and kept your mouth shut when the teacher said, "Who can name all fifty states?" you had a pretty good chance to stay clear of Imogene.

As far as anyone could tell, Imogene was just like the rest of the Herdmans. She never learned anything either, except dirty words and secrets about everybody.

Twice a year we had to go to the health room to get weighed and measured, and Imogene always managed to find out exactly what everybody weighed. Sometimes she would hang around waiting for the nurse, Miss Hemphill, to give her a Band-Aid; sometimes she would sneak behind the curtain where they kept a folding cot and just stay there the whole time, with one eye on the scales.

"Why are you still here, Imogene?" Miss Hemphill asked one day. "You can go back to your room."

"I think you better look and see if I've got what Ollie has."

"What does Ollie have?"

Imogene shrugged. "We don't know. Red spots all over."

Miss Hemphill looked at her. "What did the doctor say?"

"We didn't have a doctor." Imogene began scrunching her back up and down against the medicine cabinet.

"Well, does Ollie have a fever? Is he in bed?"

"No, he's in the first grade."

"Right now?" Miss Hemphill stared. "Why, he shouldn't be in school with red spots! It could be measles or chicken pox . . . any number of things . . . contagious things. What are you doing?"

"Scratching my back," Imogene said. "Boy, do I itch!"

"The rest of you boys and girls go back to your classroom," Miss Hemphill said, "and, Imogene, you stay right here."

So we all went back to our room, and Miss Hemphill went to the first grade to look at Ollie, and Imogene stayed in the health room and copied down everybody's weight from Miss Hemphill's records.

Your weight was supposed to be a big secret, like what you got on your report card.

"It's nobody's business what you get on your report card," all the teachers said. And Miss Hemphill said the same thing—"It's nobody's business what you weigh."

Not even the fat kids could find out what they weighed, but Imogene always knew.

"Don't let Albert Pelfrey on the swing!" she would yell at recess. "He'll bust it. Albert Pelfrey weighs a hundred and forty-three pounds. Last time he weighed a hundred and thirty-seven." So right away everybody knew two things about Albert—we knew exactly how fat he was, and we also knew that he was getting fatter all the time.

"You have to go to fat-camp this summer," Imogene hollered at him. "Miss Hemphill wrote it down on your paper."

Fat-camp is a place where they feed you lettuce and grapefruit and cottage cheese and eggs for a month, and you either give up and cheat or give up and get skinny.

"I am not!" Albert said. "I'm going to Disneyland with my Uncle Frank."

"That's what you think!" Imogene told him.

Albert had to believe her—she was always right about things like that—so all year he had fat-camp to look forward to instead of Disneyland.

Sometimes Imogene would blackmail the fat kids if they had anything she wanted . . . like Wanda Pierce's charm bracelet.

Wanda Pierce weighed about a ton—she even had fat eyes—and her hobby was this charm bracelet. It had twenty-two charms and every single one did something: the little wheels turned, or the little bitty piano keys went "plink," or the little tiny drawers opened and closed.

Besides being a fat kid, Wanda was also a rich kid, so every time you turned around she had a new charm.

"Look at my new charm," she would say. "It cost $6.95 without the tax. It's a bird, and when you push this little knob, its wings flutter. It cost $6.95."

They were great charms, but everybody got sick of hearing about them, so it was almost a relief when Imogene blackmailed her out of it.

"I know how much you weigh, Wanda," Imogene told her. "I wrote it down on this piece of paper. See?"

It must have been an awful amount, because even Wanda looked horrified. So Imogene got her charm bracelet, and she got Lucille Golden's imitation alligator pocketbook with "Souvenir of Florida" written on it. For a while she got ten cents a week from Floyd Brush, till Floyd caught double pneumonia and lost fifteen pounds and didn't care anymore.

My friend Alice Wendleken was so nasty-clean that she had detergent hands by the time she was four years old. Just the same, Alice picked up a case of head lice when she was at summer camp, and somehow Imogene found out about that. She would sneak up on Alice at recess and holler "Cooties!" and smack Alice's head. She nearly knocked Alice cross-eyed before one of the teachers saw her and took both of them in to the principal.

"Now, what's this all about?" the principal wanted to know, but Alice wouldn't say.

"I *had* to hit her," Imogene told him. "She's got cooties, and I saw one crawling in her hair, and I don't want them on me."

"You did not see one!" Alice said. "I don't have them anymore!"

"What do you mean, you don't have them anymore?" the principal said. "Did you have them *lately?*" It really shook him up—he didn't want a whole school full of kids with cooties. So he sent Alice to the health room and the nurse went all through her head with a fine-tooth comb and a magnifying glass, and finally said it was all right.

But it was too late—everybody called Alice "Cooties" the whole rest of the year.

If Imogene didn't know a secret about a person, she would make one up. She would catch you in the girls' room or out in the hall and whisper, "I know what you did!" and then you'd go crazy trying to figure out what it was you did that Imogene knew about.

It was no good trying to get secrets on the Herd-

mans. Everybody already knew about the awful things they did. You couldn't even tease them about their parents, or holler "Your father's in jail!" because they didn't care. Actually, they didn't know what their father was or where he was or anything about him, because when Gladys was two years old he climbed on a railroad train and disappeared. Nobody blamed him.

Now and then you'd see Mrs. Herdman, walking the cat on a length of chain around the block. But she worked double shifts at the shoe factory, and wasn't home much.

My mother's friend, Miss Philips, was a social-service worker and she tried to get some welfare money for the Herdmans, so Mrs. Herdman could just work one shift and spend more time with her children. But Mrs. Herdman wouldn't do it; she liked the work, she said.

"It's not the work," Miss Philips told my mother, "and it's not the money. It's just that she'd rather be at the shoe factory than shut up at home with that crowd of kids." She sighed. "I can't say I blame her."

So the Herdmans pretty much looked after themselves. Ralph looked after Imogene, and Imogene looked after Leroy, and Leroy looked after Claude and so on down the line. The Herdmans were like most big families—the big ones taught the little ones everything they knew . . . and the proof of that was that the meanest Herdman of all was Gladys, the youngest.

We figured they were headed straight for hell, by way of the state penitentiary . . . until they got themselves mixed up with the church, and my mother, and our Christmas pageant.

2

Mother didn't expect to have anything to do with the Christmas pageant except to make me and my little brother Charlie be in it (we didn't want to) and to make my father go and see it (he didn't want to).

Every year he said the same thing—"I've seen the Christmas pageant."

"You haven't seen this year's Christmas pageant," Mother would tell him. "Charlie is a shepherd this year."

"Charlie was a shepherd last year. No . . . you go on and go. I'm just going to put on my bathrobe and sit by the fire and relax. There's never anything different about the Christmas pageant."

"There's something different this year," Mother said.

"What?"

"Charlie is wearing your bathrobe."

So that year my father went . . . to see his bathrobe, he said.

Actually, he went every year but it was always a struggle, and Mother said that was her contribution to the Christmas pageant—getting my father to go to it.

But then she got stuck with the whole thing when Mrs. George Armstrong fell and broke her leg.

We knew about this as soon as it happened, because Mrs. Armstrong only lived a block and a half away. We heard the siren and saw the ambulance and watched the policemen carry her out of the house on a stretcher.

"Call Mr. Armstrong at his work!" she yelled at the policemen. "Shut off the stove under my potatoes! Inform the Ladies' Aid that I won't be at the meeting!"

One of the neighbor women called out, "Helen, are you in much pain?" and Mrs. Armstrong yelled back, "Yes, terrible! Don't let those children tear up my privet hedge!"

Even in pain, Mrs. Armstrong could still give orders. She was so good at giving orders that she was just naturally the head of anything she belonged to, and at church she did everything but preach. Most of all, she ran the Christmas pageant every year. And here she was, two weeks before Thanksgiving, flat on her back.

"I don't know what they'll do now about the pageant," Mother said.

But the pageant wasn't the only problem. Mrs. Armstrong was also chairman of the Ladies' Aid Bazaar, and coordinator of the Women's Society Pot-luck Supper, and there was a lot of telephoning back and forth to see who would take over those jobs.

Mother had a list of names, and while she was calling people about the Ladies' Aid Bazaar, Mrs. Homer McCarthy was trying to call Mother about the pot-luck supper. But Mrs. McCarthy got somebody else to do that, and Mother got somebody else to do the bazaar. So the only thing left was the Christmas pageant.

And Mother got stuck with that.

"I could run the pot-luck supper with one hand tied behind my back," Mother told us. "All you have to do is make sure everybody doesn't bring meat loaf. But the Christmas pageant!"

Our Christmas pageant isn't what you'd call four-star entertainment. Mrs. Armstrong breaking her leg was the only unexpected thing that ever happened to it. The script is standard (the inn, the stable, the shepherds, the star), and so are the costumes, and so is the casting.

Primary kids are angels; intermediate kids are

17

shepherds; big boys are Wise Men; Elmer Hopkins, the minister's son, has been Joseph for as long as I can remember; and my friend Alice Wendleken is Mary because she's so smart, so neat and clean, and, most of all, so holy-looking.

All the rest of us are the angel choir—lined up according to height because nobody can sing parts. As a matter of fact, nobody can *sing*. We're strictly a no-talent outfit except for a girl named Alberta Bottles, who whistles. Last year Alberta whistled "What Child Is This?" for a change of pace, but nobody liked it, especially Mrs. Bottles, because Alberta put too much into it and ran out of air and passed out cold on the manger in the middle of the third verse.

Aside from that, though, it's always just the Christmas story, year after year, with people shuffling around in bathrobes and bedsheets and sharp wings.

"Well," my father said, once Mother got put in charge of it, "here's your big chance. Why don't you cancel the pageant and show movies?"

"Movies of what?" Mother said.

"I don't know. Fred Stamper has five big reels of Yellowstone National Park."

"What does Yellowstone National Park have to do with Christmas?" Mother asked.

"I know a good movie," Charlie said. "We had

it at school. It shows a heart operation, and two kids got sick."

"Never mind," Mother said. "I guess you all think you're pretty funny, but the Christmas pageant is a tradition, and I don't plan to do anything different."

Of course nobody even thought about the Herdmans in connection with the Christmas pageant. Most of us spent all week in school being pounded and poked and pushed around by Herdmans, and we looked forward to Sunday as a real day of rest.

Once a month the whole Sunday school would go to church for the first fifteen minutes of the service and do something special—sing a song, or act out a parable, or recite Bible verses. Usually the little kids sang "Jesus Loves Me," which was all they were up to.

But when my brother Charlie was in with the little kids, his teacher thought up something different to do. She had everybody write down on a piece of paper what they liked best about Sunday school, or draw a picture of what they liked best. And when we all got in the church she stood up in front of the congregation and said, "Today some of our youngest boys and girls are going to tell you what Sunday school means to them. Betsy, what do you have on your paper?"

Betsy Cathcart stood up and said, "What I like

19

best about Sunday school is the good feeling I get when I go there."

I don't think she wrote that down at all, but it sounded terrific, of course.

One kid said he liked hearing all the Bible stories. Another kid said, "I like learning songs about Jesus."

Eight or nine little kids stood up and said what they liked, and it was always something good about Jesus or God or cheerful friends or the nice teacher.

Finally the teacher said, "I think we have time for one more. Charlie, what can you tell us about Sunday school?"

My little brother Charlie stood up and he didn't even have to look at his piece of paper. "What I like best about Sunday school," he said, "is that there aren't any Herdmans here."

Well. The teacher should have stuck with "Jesus Loves Me," because everybody forgot all the nice churchy things the other kids said, and just remembered what Charlie said about the Herdmans.

When we went to pick him up after church his teacher told us, "I'm sure there are many things that Charlie likes about Sunday school. Maybe he will tell you what some of them are." She smiled at all of us, but you could tell she was really mad.

On the way home I asked Charlie, "What are some of the other things you like that she was talking about?"

He shrugged. "I like all the other stuff but she said to write down what we liked best, and what I like best is no Herdmans."

"Not a very Christian sentiment," my father said.

"Maybe not, but it's a very practical one," Mother told him—last year Charlie had spent the whole second grade being black-and-blue because he had to sit next to Leroy Herdman.

In the end it was Charlie's fault that the Herdmans showed up in church.

For three days in a row Leroy Herdman stole the dessert from Charlie's lunch box and finally Charlie just gave up trying to do anything about it. "Oh, go on and take it," he said. "I don't care. I get all the dessert I want in Sunday school."

Leroy wanted to know more about that. "What kind of dessert?" he said.

"Chocolate cake," Charlie told him, " and candy bars and cookies and Kool-Aid. We get refreshments all the time, all we want."

"You're a liar," Leroy said.

Leroy was right. We got jelly beans at Easter and punch and cookies on Children's Day, and that was it.

"We get ice cream, too," Charlie went on, "and doughnuts and popcorn balls."

"Who gives it to you?" Leroy wanted to know.

"The minister," Charlie said. He didn't know who else to say.

21

Of course that was the wrong thing to tell Herdmans if you wanted them to stay away. And sure enough, the very next Sunday there they were, slouching into Sunday school, eyes peeled for the refreshments.

"Where do you get the cake?" Ralph asked the Sunday-school superintendent, and Mr. Grady said, "Well, son, I don't know about any cake, but they're collecting the food packages out in the kitchen." What he meant was the canned stuff we brought in every year as a Thanksgiving present for the Orphans Home.

It was just our bad luck that the Herdmans picked that Sunday to come, because when they saw all the cans of spaghetti and beans and grape drink and peanut butter, they figured there might be some truth to what Charlie said about refreshments.

So they stayed. They didn't sing any hymns or say any prayers, but they did make a little money, because I saw Imogene snake a handful of coins out of the collection basket when it went past her.

At the end of the morning Mr. Grady came to every class and made an announcement.

"We'll be starting rehearsals soon for our Christmas pageant," he said, "and next week after the service we'll all gather in the back of the church to decide who will play the main roles. But of course we want every boy and girl in our Sunday school to take part in the pageant, so be sure your parents know that you'll be staying a little later next Sunday."

Mr. Grady made this same speech every year, so he didn't get any wild applause. Besides, as I said, we all knew what part we were going to play anyway.

Alice Wendleken must have been a little bit worried, though, because she turned around to me with this sticky smile on her face and said, "I hope you're going to be in the angel choir again. You're so good in the angel choir."

What she meant was, I hope you won't get to be Mary just because your mother's running the pageant. She didn't have to worry. I didn't want to be Mary. I didn't want to be in the angel choir either, but everybody had to be something.

All of a sudden Imogene Herdman dug me in the ribs with her elbow. She has the sharpest elbows of anybody I ever knew. "What's the pageant?" she said.

"It's a play," I said, and for the first time that day (except when she saw the collection basket) Imogene looked interested. All the Herdmans are big moviegoers, though they never pay their own way. One or two of them start a fight at the box office of the theater while the others slip in. They get their popcorn the same way, and then they spread out all over the place so the manager can never find them all before the picture's over.

"What's the play about?" Imogene asked.

"It's about Jesus," I said.

"Everything here is," she muttered, so I figured Imogene didn't care much about the Christmas pageant.

But I was wrong.

24

3

Mrs. Armstrong, who was still trying to run things from her hospital bed, said that the same people always got the main parts. "But it's important to give everybody a chance," she told Mother over the telephone. "Let me tell you what I do."

Mother sighed, and turned off the heat under the pork chops. "All right, Helen," she said.

Mrs. Armstrong called Mother at least every other day, and she always called at suppertime. "Don't let me interrupt your supper," she always said, and then went right ahead and did it anyway, while my father paced up and down the hall, saying things under his breath about Mrs. Armstrong.

"Here's what I do," Mrs. Armstrong said. "I get them all together and tell them about the rehearsals,

25

and that they must be on time and pay close attention. Then I tell them that the main parts are Mary and Joseph and the Wise Men and the Angel of the Lord. And then I always remind them that there are no small parts, only small actors."

"Do they understand what that means?" Mother asked.

"Oh, yes," Mrs. Armstrong said.

Later Mother asked me if I knew what that meant, about small parts and small actors.

I didn't really know—none of us did. It was just something Mrs. Armstrong always said. "I guess it means that the short kids have to be in the front row of the angel choir, or else nobody can see them."

"I thought so," Mother said. "It doesn't mean that at all. It really means that every single person in the pageant is just as important as every other person—that the littlest baby angel is just as important as Mary."

"Go and tell that to Alice Wendleken," I said, and Mother told me not to be so fresh. She didn't get very mad, though, because she knew I was right. You could have a Christmas pageant without *any* baby angels, but you couldn't have one without a Mary.

Mrs. Armstrong knew it too. "I always start with Mary," she told Mother over the telephone. "I tell them that we must choose our Mary carefully, because Mary was the mother of Jesus."

"I know that," Mother said, wanting to get off the telephone and cook the pork chops.

"Yes. I tell them that our Mary should be a cheerful, happy little girl who is unselfish and kind to others. Then I tell them about Joseph, that he was God's choice to be Jesus' father, and our Joseph ought to be a little boy . . ." She went on and on and got as far as the second Wise Man when Mother said, "Helen, I'll have to go now. There's somebody at the door."

Actually there was somebody at the door. It was my father, standing out on the porch in his coat and hat, leaning on the doorbell.

When Mother let him in he took off his hat and bowed to her. "Lady, can you give me some supper? I haven't had a square meal in three days."

"Oh, for goodness sake," Mother said, "Come on in. What will the neighbors think, to see you standing out there ringing your own doorbell? And why didn't you ring the doorbell ten minutes ago?"

Mrs. Armstrong called Mother two more times that week—to tell her that people could hem up costumes, but couldn't cut them—and to tell her not to let the angel choir wear lipstick. And by Sunday, Mother was already sick of the whole thing.

After church we all filed into the back seven pews, along with two or three Sunday-school teachers who were supposed to keep everybody quiet. It was a terrible time to try to keep everybody quiet —all the little kids were tired and all the big kids were hungry, and all the mothers wanted to go home and cook dinner, and all the fathers wanted to go home and watch the football game on TV.

"Now, this isn't going to take very long," Mother told us. My father had said it better not take very long, because he wanted to watch the football game too. He also wanted to eat, he said—he hadn't had a decent meal all week.

"First I'm going to tell you about the rehearsals," Mother said. "We'll have our rehearsals on Wednesdays at 6:30. We're only going to have five rehearsals so you must all try to be present at every one."

"What if we get sick?" asked a little kid in the front pew.

"You won't get sick," Mother told him, which was exactly what she told Charlie that morning whe Charlie said he didn't want to be a shepherd and would be sick to his stomach if she made him be one.

"Now you little children in the cradle room and the primary class will be our angels," Mother said. "You'll like that, won't you?"

They all said yes. What else could they say?

"The older boys and girls will be shepherds and guests at the inn and members of the choir." Mother was really zipping along, and I thought how mad Mrs. Armstrong would be about all the things she was leaving out.

"And we need Mary and Joseph, the three Wise Men, and the Angel of the Lord. They aren't hard parts, but they're very important parts, so those people must absolutely come to every rehearsal."

"What if *they* get sick?" It was the same little kid, and it made you wonder what kind of little kid he was, to be so interested in sickness.

"They won't get sick either," Mother said, looking a little cross. "Now, we all know what kind of person Mary was. She was quiet and gentle and kind, and the little girl who plays Mary should try to be that kind of person. I know that many of you would like to be Mary in our pageant, but of course we can only have one Mary. So I'll ask for volunteers, and then we'll all decide together which girl should get the part." That was pretty safe to say, since the only person who ever raised her hand was Alice Wendleken.

But Alice just sat there, chewing on a piece of her hair and looking down at the floor . . . and the only person who raised her hand this time was Imogene Herdman.

"Did you have a question, Imogene?" Mother asked. I guess that was the only reason she could think of for Imogene to have her hand up.

"No," Imogene said. "I want to be Mary." She

looked back over her shoulder. "And Ralph wants to be Joseph."

"Yeh," Ralph said.

Mother just stared at them. It was like a detective movie, when the nice little old gray-haired lady sticks a gun in the bank window and says "Give me all your money" and you can't believe it. Mother couldn't believe this.

"Well," she said after a minute, "we want to be sure that everyone has a chance. Does anyone else want to volunteer for Joseph?"

No one did. No one ever did, especially not Elmer Hopkins. But he couldn't do anything about it, because he was the minister's son. One year he didn't volunteer to be Joseph and neither did anyone else, and afterward I heard Reverend Hopkins talking to Elmer out in the hall.

"You're going to be Joseph," Reverend Hopkins said. "That's it."

"I don't want to be Joseph," Elmer told him. "I'm too big, and I feel dumb up there, and all those little kids give me a pain in the neck."

"I can understand that," Reverend Hopkins said. "I can even sympathize, but till somebody else volunteers for Joseph, you're stuck with it."

"Nobody's ever going to do that!" Elmer said. "I even offered Grady Baker fifty cents to be Joseph and he wouldn't do it. I'm going to have to be Joseph for the rest of my life!"

"Cheer up," Reverend Hopkins told him. "Maybe somebody will turn up."

I'll bet he didn't think the somebody would be Ralph Herdman.

"All right," Mother said, "Ralph will be our Joseph. Now, does anyone else want to volunteer for Mary?" Mother looked all around, trying to catch somebody's eye—*anybody's* eye. "Janet? . . . Roberta? . . . Alice, don't you want to volunteer this year?"

"No," Alice said, so low you could hardly hear her. "I don't want to."

Nobody volunteered to be Wise Men either, except, Leroy, Claude, and Ollie Herdman.

So there was my mother, stuck with a Christmas pageant full of Herdmans in the main roles.

There was one Herdman left over, and one main role left over, and you didn't have to be very smart to figure out that Gladys was going to be the Angel of the Lord.

"What do I have to do?" Gladys wanted to know.

"The Angel of the Lord was the one who brought the good news to the shepherds," Mother said.

Right away all the shepherds began to wiggle around in their seats, figuring that any good news Gladys brought them would come with a smack in the teeth.

Charlie's friend Hobie Carmichael raised his hand

32

and said, "I can't be a shepherd. We're going to Philadelphia."

"Why didn't you say so before?" Mother asked.

"I forgot."

Another kid said, "My mother doesn't want me to be a shepherd."

"Why not?" Mother said.

"I don't know. She just said don't be a shepherd."

One kid was honest. "Gladys Herdman hits too hard," he said.

"Why, Gladys isn't going to hit anybody!" Mother said. "What an idea! The Angel just visits the shepherds in the fields and tells them Jesus is born."

"And hits 'em," said the kid.

Of course he was right. You could just picture Gladys whamming shepherds left and right, but Mother said that was perfectly ridiculous.

"I don't want to hear another word about it," she said. "No shepherds may quit—or get sick," she added, before the kid in the front pew could ask.

While everybody was leaving, Mother grabbed Alice Wendleken by the arm and said, "Alice, why in the world didn't you raise your hand to be Mary?"

"I don't know," Alice said, looking mad.

But I knew—I'd heard Imogene Herdman telling Alice what would happen to her if she dared to volunteer: all the ordinary, everyday Herdman-things like clonking you on the head, and drawing pictures all over your homework papers, and putting worms in your coat pocket.

"I don't care," Alice told her. "I don't care what you do. I'm always Mary in the pageant."

"And next spring," Imogene went on, squinching up her eyes, "when the pussy willows come out, I'll stick a pussy willow so far down your ear that nobody can reach it—and it'll sprout there, and it'll grow and grow, and you'll spend the rest of your life with a pussy-willow bush growing out your ear."

You had to admire her—that was the worst thing any of them ever thought up to do. Of course some people might not think that could happen, but it could. Ollie Herdman did it once. He got this terrible earache in school, and when the nurse looked down his ear with her little lighted tube she yelled so loud you could hear her all the way down the hall. "He's got something growing down there!" she hollered.

They had to take Ollie to the hospital and put him under and dig this sprouted pussy willow out of his ear.

So that was why Alice kept her mouth shut about being Mary.

"You know she wouldn't do all those things she said," I told Alice as we walked home.

"Yes, she would," Alice said. "Herdmans will do anything. But your mother should have told them no. Somebody should put Imogene out of the pageant, and all the rest of them too. They'll do something terrible and ruin the whole thing."

I thought she was probably right, and so did lots of other people, and for two or three days all anybody could talk about was the Herdmans being Mary and Joseph and all.

Mrs. Homer McCarthy called Mother to say that she had been thinking and thinking about it, and if the Herdmans wanted to participate in our Christmas celebration, why didn't we let them hand out programs at the door?

"We don't have programs for the Christmas pageant," Mother said.

"Well, maybe we ought to get some printed and put the Herdmans in charge of that."

Alice's mother told the Ladies' Aid that it was sacrilegious to let Imogene Herdman be Mary. Somebody we never heard of called up Mother on the telephone and said her name was Hazelbeck and she lived on Sproul Hill, and was it true that Imogene Herdman was going to be Mary the mother of Jesus in a church play?

"Yes," Mother said. "Imogene is going to be Mary in our Christmas pageant."

"And the rest of them too?" the lady asked.

"Yes, Ralph is going to be Joseph and the others are the Wise Men and the Angel of the Lord."

"You must be crazy," this Mrs. Hazelbeck told

Mother. "I live next door to that outfit with their yelling and screaming and their insane cat and their garage door going up and down, up and down all day long, and let me tell you, you're in for a rowdy time!"

Some people said it wasn't fair for a whole family who didn't even go to our church to barge in and take over the pageant. My father said somebody better lock up the Women's Society's silver service. My mother just said she would rather be in the hospital with Mrs. Armstrong.

But then the flower committee took a potted geranium to Mrs. Armstrong and told her what was going on and she nearly fell out of bed, traction bars and all. "I feel personally responsible," she said. "Whatever happens, I accept the blame. If I'd been up and around and doing my duty, this never would have happened."

And that made my mother so mad she couldn't see straight.

"If she'd been up and around it wouldn't have happened!" Mother said. "That woman! She must be surprised that the sun is still coming up every morning without her to supervise the sunrise. Well, let me tell you—"

"Don't tell me," my father said. "I'm on your side."

"I just mean that Helen Armstrong is not the only woman alive who can run a Christmas pageant.

Up till now I'd made up my mind just to do the best I could under the circumstances, but now—" She stabbed a meat fork into the pot roast. "I'm going to make this the very best Christmas pageant anybody ever saw, and I'm going to do it with Herdmans, too. After all, they raised their hands and nobody else did. And that's that."

And it was too. For one thing, nobody else wanted to take over the pageant, with or without Herdmans; and for another thing, Reverend Hopkins got fed up with all the complaints and told everybody where to get off.

Of course, he didn't say "Go jump in the lake, Mrs. Wendleken" or anything like that. He just reminded everyone that when Jesus said "Suffer the little children to come unto me" Jesus meant all the little children, including Herdmans.

So that shut everybody up, even Alice's mother, and the next Wednesday we started rehearsals.

4

The first pageant rehearsal was usually about as much fun as a three-hour ride on the school bus, and just as noisy and crowded. This rehearsal, though, was different. Everybody shut up and settled down right away, for fear of missing something awful that the Herdmans might do.

They got there ten minutes late, sliding into the room like a bunch of outlaws about to shoot up a saloon. When Leroy passed Charlie he knuckled him behind the ear, and one little primary girl yelled as Gladys went by. But Mother had said she was going to ignore everything except blood, and since the primary kid wasn't bleeding, and neither was Charlie, nothing happened.

Mother said, "And here's the Herdman family.

We're glad to see you all," which was probably the biggest lie ever said right out loud in the church.

Imogene smiled—the Herdman smile, we called it, sly and sneaky—and there they sat, the closest thing to criminals that we knew about, and they were going to represent the best and most beautiful. No wonder everybody was so worked up.

Mother started to separate everyone into angels and shepherds and guests at the inn, but right away she ran into trouble.

"Who were the shepherds?" Leroy Herdman wanted to know. "Where did they come from?"

Ollie Herdman didn't even know what a shepherd was . . . or, anyway, that's what he said.

"What was the inn?" Claude asked. "What's an inn?"

"It's like a motel," somebody told him, "where people go to spend the night."

"What people?" Claude said. "Jesus?"

"Oh, honestly!" Alice Wendleken grumbled. "Jesus wasn't even born yet! Mary and Joseph went there."

"Why?" Ralph asked.

"What happened first?" Imogene hollered at my mother. "Begin at the beginning!"

That really scared me because the beginning would be the Book of Genesis, where it says "In the beginning . . ." and if we were going to have to start with the Book of Genesis we'd never get through.

The thing was, the Herdmans didn't know anything about the Christmas story. They knew that Christmas was Jesus' birthday, but everything else was news to them—the shepherds, the Wise Men, the star, the stable, the crowded inn.

It was hard to believe. At least, it was hard for me to believe—Alice Wendleken said she didn't have any trouble believing it. "How would they find out about the Christmas story?" she said. "They don't even know what a Bible is. Look what Gladys did to that Bible last week."

While Imogene was snitching money from the collection plate in my class, Gladys and Ollie drew mustaches and tails on all the disciples in the primary-grade Illustrated Bible.

"They never went to church in their whole life till your little brother told them we got refreshments," Alice said, "and all you ever hear about Christmas in school is how to make ornaments out of aluminum foil. So how would they know about the Christmas story?"

She was right. Of course they might have read about it, but they never read anything except "Amazing Comics." And they might have heard about it on TV, except that Ralph paid sixty-five cents for their TV at a garage sale, and you couldn't see anything on it unless somebody held onto the antenna. Even then, you couldn't see much.

The only other way for them to hear about the Christmas story was from their parents, and I guess Mr. Herdman never got around to it before he climbed on the railroad train. And it was pretty clear that Mrs. Herdman had given up ever trying to tell them anything.

So they just didn't know. And Mother said she had better begin by reading the Christmas story from the Bible. This was a pain in the neck to most of us because we knew the whole thing backward and forward and never had to be told anything except who we were supposed to be, and where we were supposed to stand.

". . . Joseph and Mary, his espoused wife, being great with child . . ."

"Pregnant!" yelled Ralph Herdman.

Well. That stirred things up. All the big kids began to giggle and all the little kids wanted to know what was so funny, and Mother had to hammer on the floor with a blackboard pointer. "That's enough, Ralph," she said, and went on with the story.

"I don't think it's very nice to say Mary was pregnant," Alice whispered to me.

"But she was," I pointed out. In a way, though, I agreed with her. It sounded too ordinary. Anybody could be pregnant. "Great with child" sounded better for Mary.

"I'm not supposed to talk about people being pregnant." Alice folded her hands in her lap and pinched her lips together. "I'd better tell my mother."

"Tell her what?"

"That your mother is talking about things like that in church. My mother might not want me to be here."

I was pretty sure she would do it. She wanted to be Mary, and she was mad at Mother. I knew, too, that she would make it sound worse than it was and Mrs. Wendleken would get madder than she already was. Mrs. Wendleken didn't even want cats to have kittens or birds to lay eggs, and she wouldn't let Alice play with anybody who had two rabbits.

But there wasn't much I could do about it, except pinch Alice, which I did. She yelped, and Mother separated us and made me sit beside Imogene Herdman and sent Alice to sit in the middle of the baby angels.

I wasn't crazy to sit next to Imogene—after all, I'd spent my whole life staying away from Imogene —but she didn't even notice me . . . not much, anyway.

"Shut up," was all she said. "I want to hear her."

I couldn't believe it. Among other things, the Herdmans were famous for never sitting still and never paying attention to anyone—teachers, parents (their own or anybody else's), the truant officer, the police—yet here they were, eyes glued on my mother and taking in every word.

"What's that?" they would yell whenever they didn't understand the language, and when Mother read about there being no room at the inn, Imogene's jaw dropped and she sat up in her seat.

"My God!" she said. "Not even for Jesus?"

I saw Alice purse her lips together so I knew that was something else Mrs. Wendleken would hear about—swearing in the church.

"Well, now, after all," Mother explained, "nobody knew the baby was going to turn out to be Jesus."

"You said Mary knew," Ralph said. "Why didn't she tell them?"

"*I* would have told them!" Imogene put in. "Boy, would I have told them! What was the matter with Joseph that he didn't tell them? Her pregnant and everything," she grumbled.

"What was that they laid the baby in?" Leroy said. "That manger . . . is that like a bed? Why would they have a bed in the barn?"

"That's just the point," Mother said. "They *didn't* have a bed in the barn, so Mary and Joseph had to use whatever there was. What would you do if you had a new baby and no bed to put the baby in?"

"We put Gladys in a bureau drawer," Imogene volunteered.

"Well, there you are," Mother said, blinking a little. "You didn't have a bed for Gladys so you had to use something else."

"Oh, we had a bed," Ralph said, "only Ollie was still in it and he wouldn't get out. He didn't like Gladys." He elbowed Ollie. "Remember how you didn't like Gladys?"

I thought that was pretty smart of Ollie, not to like Gladys right off the bat.

"*Anyway*," Mother said, "Mary and Joseph used the manger. A manger is a large wooden feeding trough for animals."

"What were the wadded-up clothes?" Claude wanted to know.

"The what?" Mother said.

"You read about it—'she wrapped him in wadded-up clothes.' "

"*Swaddling* clothes." Mother sighed. "Long ago, people used to wrap their babies very tightly in big pieces of material, so they couldn't move around. It made the babies feel cozy and comfortable."

I thought it probably just made the babies mad. Till then, I didn't know what swaddling clothes were either, and they sounded terrible. so I wasn't too surprised when Imogene got all excited about that.

"You mean they tied him up and put him in a feedbox?" she said. "Where was the Child Welfare?"

44

The Child Welfare was always checking up on the Herdmans. I'll bet if the Child Welfare had ever found Gladys all tied up in a bureau drawer they would have done something about it.

"And, lo, the Angel of the Lord came upon them," Mother went on, "and the glory of the Lord shone round about them, and—"

"Shazam!" Gladys yelled, flinging her arms out and smacking the kid next to her.

"What?" Mother said. Mother never read "Amazing Comics."

"Out of the black night with horrible vengeance, the Mighty Marvo—"

"I don't know what you're talking about, Gladys," Mother said. "This is the Angel of the Lord who comes to the shepherds in the fields, and—"

"Out of nowhere, right?" Gladys said. "In the black night, right?"

"Well . . ." Mother looked unhappy. "In a way."

So Gladys sat back down, looking very satisfied, as if this was at least one part of the Christmas story that made sense to her.

"Now when Jesus was born in Bethlehem of Judaea," Mother went on reading, "behold there came Wise Men from the East to Jerusalem, saying—"

"That's you, Leroy," Ralph said, "and Claude and Ollie. So pay attention."

"What does it mean, Wise Men?" Ollie wanted

to know. "Were they like schoolteachers?"

"No, dumbbell," Claude said. "It means like President of the United States."

Mother looked surprised, and a little pleased—like she did when Charlie finally learned the timestables up to five. "Why, that's very close, Claude," she said. "Actually, they were kings."

"Well, it's about time," Imogene muttered. "Maybe they'll tell the innkeeper where to get off, and get the baby out of the barn."

"They saw the young child with Mary, his mother, and fell down and worshipped him, and presented unto him gifts: gold, and frankincense, and myrrh."

"What's that stuff?" Leroy wanted to know.

"Precious oils," Mother said, "and fragrant resins."

"Oil!" Imogene hollered. "What kind of a cheap king hands out oil for a present? You get better presents from the firemen!"

Sometimes the Herdmans got Christmas presents at the Firemen's Party, but the Santa Claus always had to feel all around the packages to be sure they weren't getting bows and arrows or dart guns or anything like that. Imogene usually got sewing cards or jigsaw puzzles and she never liked them, but I guess she figured they were better than oil.

Then we came to King Herod, and the Herdmans never heard of him either, so Mother had to explain that it was Herod who sent the Wise Men to find the baby Jesus.

"Was it him that sent the crummy presents?" Ollie wanted to know, and Mother said it was worse than that—he planned to have the baby Jesus put to death.

"My God!" Imogene said. "He just got born and already they're out to kill him!"

The Herdmans wanted to know all about Herod —what he looked like, and how rich he was, and whether he fought wars with people.

"He must have been the main king," Claude said, "if he could make the other three do what he wanted them to."

"If I was a king," Leroy said, "I wouldn't let some other king push me around."

"You couldn't help it if he was the main king."

"I'd go be king somewhere else."

They were really interested in Herod, and I figured they liked him. He was so mean he could have been their ancestor—Herod Herdman. But I was wrong.

"Who's going to be Herod in this play?" Leroy said.

"We don't show Herod in our pageant," Mother said. And they all got mad. They wanted somebody to be Herod so they could beat up on him.

I couldn't understand the Herdmans. You would have thought the Christmas story came right out of the F.B.I. files, they got so involved in it—wanted a bloody end to Herod, worried about Mary having her baby in a barn, and called the Wise Men a bunch of dirty spies.

And they left the first rehearsal arguing about whether Joseph should have set fire to the inn, or just chased the innkeeper into the next county.

5

When we got home my father wanted to hear all about it.

"Well," Mother said, "just suppose you had never heard the Christmas story, and didn't know anything about it, and then somebody told it to you. What would you think?"

My father looked at her for a minute or two and then he said, "Well, I guess I would think it was pretty disgraceful that they couldn't find any room for a pregnant woman except in the stable."

I was amazed. It didn't seem natural for my father to be on the same side as the Herdmans. But then, it didn't seem natural for the Herdmans to be on the *right* side of a thing. It would have made more sense for them to be on Herod's side.

"Exactly," Mother said. "It was perfectly disgraceful. And I never thought about it much. You hear all about the nice warm stable with all the animals breathing, and the sweet-smelling hay—but that doesn't change the fact that they put Mary in a barn. Now, let me tell you . . ." She told my father all about the rehearsal and when she was through she said, "It's clear to me that, deep down, those children have *some* good instincts after all."

My father said he couldn't exactly agree. "According to you," he said, "their chief instinct was to burn Herod alive."

"No, their chief instinct was to get Mary and the baby out of the barn. But even so, it was *Herod* they wanted to do away with, and not Mary or Joseph. They picked out the right villain—that must mean something."

"Maybe so." My father looked up from his newspaper. "Is that what finally happened to Herod? What *did* happen to Herod, anyway?"

None of us knew. I had never thought much about Herod. He was just a name, somebody in the Bible, Herodtheking.

But the Herdmans went and looked him up.

The very next day Imogene grabbed me at recess. "How do you get a book out of the library?" she said.

"You have to have a card."

"How do you get a card?"

"You have to sign your name."

She looked at me for a minute, with her eyes all squinched up. "Do you have to sign your own name?"

I thought Imogene probably wanted to get one of the dirty books out of the basement, which is where they keep them, but I knew nobody would let her do that. There is this big chain across the stairs to the basement and Miss Graebner, the librarian, can hear it rattle no matter where she is in the library, so you don't stand a chance of getting down there.

"Sure you have to sign your own name," I said. "They have to know who has the books." I didn't see what difference it made—whether she signed the card with her own name, or signed the card Queen Elizabeth—Miss Graebner still wasn't going to let Imogene Herdman take any books out of the public library.

I guess she couldn't stop them from using the library, though, because that was where they found out about Herod.

They went in that afternoon, all six of them, and told Miss Graebner that they wanted library cards. Usually when anybody told Miss Graebner that they wanted a library card, she got this big happy smile on her face and said, "Good! We want all our boys and girls to have library cards."

She didn't say that to the Herdmans, though.

She just asked them *why* they wanted library cards.

"We want to read about Jesus," Imogene said.

"Not Jesus," Ralph said, "that king who was out to get Jesus . . . Herod."

Later on Miss Graebner told my mother that she had been a librarian for thirty-eight years and loved every minute of it because every day brought something new and different. "But now," she said, "I might as well retire. When Imogene Herdman came in and said she wanted to read about Jesus, I knew I'd heard everything there was to hear."

At the next rehearsal Mother started, again, to separate everyone into angels and shepherds and guests at the inn but she didn't get very far. The Herdmans wanted to rewrite the whole pageant and hang Herod for a finish. They couldn't stand it that he died in bed of old age.

"It wasn't just Jesus he was after," Ralph told us. "He killed all kinds of people."

"He even killed his own wife," Leroy said.

"And nothing happened to him," Imogene grumbled.

"Well, he died, didn't he?" somebody said. "Maybe he died a horrible death. What did he die of?"

Ralph shrugged. "It didn't say. Flu, I guess."

They were so mad about it that I thought they might quit the pageant. But they didn't—not then or ever—and all the people who kept hoping that the Herdmans would get bored and leave were out

of luck. They showed up at rehearsals, right on time, and did just what they were supposed to do.

But they were still Herdmans, and there was at least one person who didn't forget that for a minute.

One day I saw Alice Wendleken writing something down on a little pad of paper, and trying to hide it with her other hand.

"It's none of your business," she said.

It *wasn't* any of my business, but it wasn't any of Alice's, either. What she wrote was "Gladys Herdman drinks communion wine."

"It isn't wine," I said. "It's grape juice."

"I don't care what it is, she drinks it. I've seen her three times with her mouth all purple. They steal crayons from the Sunday-school cupboards, too, and if you shake the Happy Birthday bank in the kindergarten room it doesn't make a sound. They stole all the pennies out of that."

I was amazed at Alice. I would never think to go and shake the Happy Birthday bank.

"And every time you go in the girls' room," she went on, "the whole air is blue, and Imogene Herdman is sitting there in the Mary costume, smoking cigars!"

Alice wrote all these things down, and how many times each thing happened. I don't know why, unless it made her feel good to see, in black and white, just how awful they were.

Since none of the Herdmans had ever gone to church or Sunday school or read the Bible or anything, they didn't know how things were supposed to be. Imogene, for instance, didn't know that Mary was supposed to be acted out in one certain way—sort of quiet and dreamy and out of this world.

The way Imogene did it, Mary was a lot like Mrs. Santoro at the Pizza Parlor. Mrs. Santoro is a big fat lady with a little skinny husband and nine children and she yells and hollers and hugs her kids and slaps them around. That's how Imogene's Mary was—loud and bossy.

"Get away from the baby!" she yelled at Ralph, who was Joseph. And she made the Wise Men keep their distance.

"The Wise Men want to honor the Christ Child," Mother explained, for the tenth time. "They don't mean to harm him, for heaven's sake!"

But the Wise Men didn't know how things were supposed to be either, and nobody blamed Imogene for shoving them out of the way. You got the feeling that *these* Wise Men were going to hustle back to Herod as fast as they could and squeal on the baby, out of pure meanness.

They thought about it, too.

"What if we *didn't* go home another way?" Leroy demanded. Leroy was Melchior. "What if we went back to the king and told on the baby—where he was and all?"

"He would murder Jesus," Ralph said. "Old Herod would murder him."

"He would not!" That was Imogene, with fire in her eye, and since the Herdmans fought one another just as fast as they fought everybody else, Mother had to step in and settle everyone down.

I thought about it later though and I decided that if Herod, a king, set out to murder Jesus, a carpenter's baby son, he would surely find some way to do it. So when Leroy said "What if we went back and told on the baby?" it gave you something to think about.

No Jesus . . . ever.

I don't know whether anybody else got this flash. Alice Wendleken, for one, didn't.

"I don't think it's very nice to talk about the baby Jesus being murdered," she said, stitching her lips together and looking sour. That was one more thing to write down on her pad of paper, and one more thing to tell her mother about the Herdmans—besides the fact that they swore and smoked and stole and all. I think she kept hoping that they would do one great big sinful thing and her mother would say, "Well, that's that!" and get on the telephone and have them thrown out.

"Be sure and tell your mother that I can step right in and be Mary if I have to," she told me as we stood in the back row of the angel choir. "And if *I'm* Mary we can get the Perkins baby for Jesus.

57

But Mrs. Perkins won't let Imogene Herdman get her hands on him." The Perkins baby would have made a terrific Jesus, and Alice knew it.

The way things stood, we didn't have any baby at all—and this really bothered my mother because you couldn't very well have the best Christmas pageant in history with the chief character missing.

We had lots of babies offered in the beginning—all the way from Eugene Sloper who was so new he was still red, up to Junior Caudill who was almost four (his mother said he could scrunch up). But when all the mothers found out about the Herdmans they withdrew their babies.

Mother had called everybody she knew, trying to scratch up a baby, but the closest she came was Bernice Watrous, who kept foster babies all the time.

"I've got a darling little boy right now," Bernice told Mother. "He's three months old, and so good I hardly know he's in the house. He'd be wonderful. Of course he's Chinese. Does that matter?"

"No," Mother said. "It doesn't matter at all."

But Bernice's baby got adopted two weeks before Christmas, and Bernice said she didn't like to ask to borrow him back right away.

So that was that.

"Listen," Imogene said. "I'll get us a baby."

"How would you do that?" Mother asked.

"I'll steal one," Imogene said. "There's always

two or three babies in carriages outside the A&P supermarket."

"Oh, Imogene, don't be ridiculous," Mother said, "You can't just walk off with somebody's baby, you know!" I doubt if Imogene *did* know that—she walked off with everything else.

"We just won't worry anymore about a baby," Mother said. "We'll use a baby doll. That'll be better anyway."

Imogene looked pleased. "A doll can't bite you," she pointed out. Which just went to prove that Herdmans started out mean, right from the cradle.

6

Our last rehearsal happened to be the night before the pot-luck supper, and when we got there the kitchen was full of ladies in aprons, counting out dishes and silverware and making applesauce cake for the dessert.

"I'm sorry about this," one of the ladies told Mother, "but with so much to do at this time of year, the committee decided to come in this evening and set up the tables and all. I just hope we won't bother you."

"Oh, you won't," Mother said. "We won't be in the kitchen. You won't even know we're here."

Mother was wrong—everybody in that end of town knew we were there before the evening was over.

"Now, this is going to be a dress rehearsal," Mother told us all, and right away three or four baby angels began hollering that they forgot their wings. Half the angel choir had forgotten their robes, and Hobie Carmichael said he didn't have any kind of a costume.

"Wear your father's bathrobe," Charlie told him. "That's what I do."

"He doesn't have a bathrobe."

"What does he hang around the house in?"

"His underwear," Hobie said.

I looked at Alice Wendleken to see if she was going to write that down on her pad of paper, but Alice was standing all by herself in a corner, patting her hair. Her hair was all washed and curled, and her robe was clean and pressed. She had even put vaseline on her eyelids, so they would shine in the candlelight and everyone would say "Who is that lovely girl in the angel choir? Why isn't she Mary?" I guess Alice was afraid to move, for fear she might spoil herself.

"Don't worry about your wings," Mother said. "The main point of a dress rehearsal isn't the costumes. The main point is to go right straight through without stopping. And that's what we're going to do, just as if we were doing it for the whole congregation. I'm going to sit in the back of the church and be the audience."

But it didn't work that way. The baby angels came

61

in at the wrong place and had to go back out again, and a whole gang of shepherds didn't come in at all, for fear of Gladys. Imogene couldn't find the baby Jesus doll, and wrapped up a great big memorial flower urn in the blanket, and then dropped it on Ralph's foot. And half the angel choir sang "Away in a Manger" while the other half sang "O, Little Town of Bethlehem."

So we had to start over a lot.

"I've got the baby here," Imogene barked at the Wise Men. "Don't touch him! I named him Jesus."

"No, no, no." Mother came flying up the aisle. "Now, Imogene, you know you're not supposed to say anything. Nobody says anything in our pageant, except the Angel of the Lord and the choir singing carols. Mary and Joseph and the Wise Men make a lovely picture for us to look at while we think about Christmas and what it means."

I guess Mother had to say things like that, even though everybody knew it was a big lie. The Herdmans didn't look like *anything* out of the Bible— more like trick-or-treat. Imogene even had on great big gold earrings, and she wouldn't take them off.

"Now, Imogene," Mother said. "You know Mary didn't wear earrings."

"I have to wear these," Imogene said.

"Why is that?"

"I got my ears pierced, and if I don't keep something in 'em, they'll grow together."

"Well, they won't grow together in an hour and a half," Mother said.

"No . . . but I better leave 'em in." Imogene pulled on her earrings, which made you shudder—it was like looking at the pictures in *National Geographic* of natives with their ears stretched all the way to their shoulders.

"What did the doctor say about leaving something in them?" Mother said.

"What doctor?"

"Well, who pierced your ears?"

"Gladys," Imogene said.

That really made you shudder—the thought of Gladys Herdman piercing ears. I thought she probably used an ice pick, and for the next six months I kept watching Imogene, to see her ears turn black and fall off.

"All right," Mother said, "but we'll try to find something smaller and more appropriate for you to wear in the pageant. Now we'll start again and go right straight through, and—"

"I think I ought to tell them what his name is," Imogene said.

"No. Besides, you remember it wasn't Mary who named the baby."

"I told you!" Ralph whacked Imogene on the back. "*I* named him."

"Joseph didn't name the baby either," Mother said. "God sent an angel to tell Mary what his name should be."

Imogene sniffed. "I would have named him Bill."

Alice Wendleken sucked in her breath, and I could hear her scratching down on her pad of paper that Imogene Herdman would have called the baby Bill instead of Jesus.

"What angel was that?" Ralph wanted to know. "Was that Gladys?"

"No," Mother said. "Gladys is the angel who comes to the shepherds with the news."

"Yeh," Gladys said. "Unto you a child is born!" she yelled at the shepherds.

"Unto *me!*" Imogene yelled back at her. "Not them, me! I'm the one that had the baby!"

"No, no, no." Mother sat down on a front pew. "That just means that Jesus belongs to everybody. Unto *all* of us a child is born. Now," she sighed. "Let's start again, and—"

"Why didn't they let Mary name her own baby?" Imogene demanded. "What did that angel do, just walk up and say, 'Name him Jesus'?"

"Yes," Mother said, because she was in a hurry to get finished.

But Alice Wendleken had to open her big mouth. "I know what the angel said," Alice piped up. "She said, 'His name shall be called Wonderful, Counselor, Mighty God, Everlasting Father, the Prince of Peace.' "

I could have hit her.

"My God!" Imogene said. "He'd never get out of the first grade if he had to write all that!"

There was a big crash at the back of the church, as if somebody dropped all the collection plates. But it wasn't the collection plates—it was Mrs. Hopkins, the minister's wife, dropping a whole tray of silverware.

"I'm sorry," she said. "I was just passing by, and I thought I'd take a peek . . ."

"Would you like to sit down and watch the rehearsal?" Mother asked.

"No-o-o." Mrs. Hopkins couldn't seem to take her eyes off Imogene. "I'd better go check on the applesauce cake."

"You didn't have to say that," I told Alice. "All that about Wonderful, Everlasting Father, and all."

"Why not?" Alice said, patting her hair. "I thought Imogene wanted to know."

By that time everyone was hot and tired, and most of the baby angels had to go to the bathroom, so Mother said we would take a five-minute recess. "And then we'll start over," she said, looking sort of hopeless, "and go right straight through without stopping, won't we?"

Well, we never did go right straight through. The

five-minute recess was a big mistake, because it stretched to fifteen minutes, and Imogene spent the whole time smoking cigars in one of the johns in the ladies' room. Then Mrs. Homer McCarthy went to the ladies' room and opened the door and smelled something funny and saw some smoke—and she ran right to the church office and called the fire department.

We were singing "Angels We Have Heard on High" when what we heard was the fire engine, pulling up on the lawn of the church, with the siren blaring and the red lights flashing. The firemen hurried in and made us all go outside, and they dragged a big hose in the front door and went looking for a fire to put out.

The street was full of baby angels crying, and shepherds climbing all over the fire truck, and firemen, and all the ladies on the pot-luck committee, and neighbors who came to see what was going on, and Reverend Hopkins who ran over from the parsonage in his pajamas and his woolly bathrobe.

Nobody knew what had happened, including the Herdmans, but I guess they figured that whatever it was, they had done it, so they left.

"Why in the world did you call the fire department?" Mother asked Mrs. McCarthy, when she finally heard the whole story.

"Because the ladies' room was full of thick smoke!"

"It couldn't have been," Mother said. "You just got excited. Didn't you know it was cigar smoke?"

Mrs. McCarthy stared at her. "No, I didn't. I don't expect to find cigar smoke in the ladies' room of the church!" She whirled around and marched back to the kitchen.

But by that time the kitchen was fuller of smoke than the ladies' room, because, while everybody was milling around in the street, all the applesauce cake burned up.

Of course the ladies on the pot-luck committee were mad about that. Mrs. McCarthy was mad, and Alice said her mother would be good and mad when she heard about it. Most of the baby angels' mothers were mad because they couldn't find out what had happened—and somebody said Mrs. Hopkins was mad because Reverend Hopkins was running around the streets in his pajamas.

It turned out to be the one great big sinful thing Alice kept hoping for.

Mrs. Wendleken read Alice's notes, got on the telephone that very night and called up everybody she could think of in the Ladies' Aid and the Women's Society. And she called most of the flower committee, and all the Sunday-school teachers, and Reverend Hopkins.

And Reverend Hopkins came to see Mother. "I can't make head or tail of it," he said. "Some people say they set fire to the ladies' room. Some people say they set fire to the kitchen. One lady told me that Imogene threw a flower pot at Ralph. Mrs. Wendleken says all they do is talk about sex and underwear."

"That was Hobie Carmichael," Mother said, "talking about underwear. And they didn't set fire to anything. The only fire was in the kitchen, where the pot-luck committee let their applesauce cake burn up."

"Well . . ." Reverend Hopkins looked unhappy. "The whole church is in an uproar. Do you think we should call off the pageant?"

"Certainly not!" Mother said. By that time she was mad, too. "Why, it's going to be the best Christmas pageant we've ever had!"

Of all the lies she'd told so far, that was the biggest, but you had to admire her. It was like General Custer saying, "Bring on the Indians!"

"Maybe so," Reverend Hopkins said. "I'm just afraid that no one will come to see it."

But he was wrong.

Everybody came . . . to see what the Herdmans would do.

7

On the night of the pageant we didn't have any supper because Mother forgot to fix it. My father said that was all right. Between Mrs. Armstrong's telephone calls and the pageant rehearsals, he didn't expect supper anymore.

"When it's all over," he said, "we'll go someplace and have hamburgers." But Mother said when it was all over she might want to go someplace and hide.

"We've never once gone through the whole thing," she said. "I don't know what's going to happen. It may be the first Christmas pageant in history where Joseph and the Wise Men get in a fight, and Mary runs away with the baby."

She might be right, I thought, and I wondered what all of us in the angel choir ought to do in case that happened. It would be dumb for us just to stand there singing about the Holy Infant if Mary had run off with him.

But nothing seemed very different at first.

There was the usual big mess all over the place—baby angels getting poked in the eye by other baby angels' wings and grumpy shepherds stumbling over their bathrobes. The spotlight swooped back and forth and up and down till it made you sick at your stomach to look at it and, as usual, whoever was playing the piano pitched "Away in a Manger" so high we could hardly hear it, let alone sing it. My father says "Away in a Manger" always starts out sounding like a closetful of mice.

But everything settled down, and at 7:30 the pageant began.

While we sang "Away in a Manger," the ushers lit candles all around the church, and the spotlight came on to be the star. So you really had to know the words to "Away in a Manger" because you couldn't see anything—not even Alice Wendleken's vaseline eyelids.

After that we sang two verses of "O, Little Town of Bethlehem," and then we were supposed to hum some more "O, Little Town of Bethlehem" while Mary and Joseph came in from a side door. Only they didn't come right away. So we hummed and hummed and hummed, which is boring and also very hard, and before long doesn't sound like any song

71

at all—more like an old refrigerator.

"I knew something like this would happen," Alice Wendleken whispered to me. "They didn't come at all! We won't have any Mary and Joseph—and now what are we supposed to do?"

I guess we would have gone on humming till we all turned blue, but we didn't have to. Ralph and Imogene were there all right, only for once they didn't come through the door pushing each other out of the way. They just stood there for a minute as if they weren't sure they were in the right place—because of the candles, I guess, and the church being full of people. They looked like the people you see on the six o'clock news—refugees, sent to wait in some strange ugly place, with all their boxes and sacks around them.

It suddenly occurred to me that this was just the way it must have been for the real Holy Family, stuck away in a barn by people who didn't much care what happened to them. They couldn't have been very neat and tidy either, but more like *this* Mary and Joseph (Imogene's veil was cockeyed as usual, and Ralph's hair stuck out all around his ears). Imogene had the baby doll but she wasn't carrying it the way she was supposed to, cradled in her arms. She had it slung up over her shoulder, and before she put it in the manger she thumped it twice on the back.

I heard Alice gasp and she poked me. "I don't

think it's very nice to burp the baby Jesus," she whispered, "as if he had colic." Then she poked me again. "Do you suppose he could have had colic?"

I said, "I don't know why not," and I didn't. He *could* have had colic, or been fussy, or hungry like any other baby. After all, that was the whole point of Jesus—that he didn't come down on a cloud like something out of "Amazing Comics," but that he was born and lived . . . a real person.

Right away we had to sing "While Shepherds Watched Their Flocks by Night"—and we had to sing very loud, because there were more shepherds than there were anything else, and they made so much noise, banging their crooks around like a lot of hockey sticks.

Next came Gladys, from behind the angel choir, pushing people out of the way and stepping on everyone's feet. Since Gladys was the only one in the pageant who had anything to say she made the most of it: "Hey! Unto you a child is born!" she hollered, as if it was, for sure, the best news in the world. And all the shepherds trembled, sore afraid —of Gladys, mainly, but it looked good anyway.

Then came three carols about angels. It took that long to get the angels in because they were all primary kids and they got nervous and cried and forgot where they were supposed to go and bent their wings in the door and things like that.

We got a little rest then, while the boys sang "We Three Kings of Orient Are," and everybody in the audience shifted around to watch the Wise Men march up the aisle.

"What have they got?" Alice whispered.

I didn't know, but whatever it was, it was heavy—Leroy almost dropped it. He didn't have his frankincense jar either, and Claude and Ollie didn't have anything although they were supposed to bring the gold and the myrrh.

"I knew this would happen," Alice said for the second time. "I bet it's something awful."

"Like what?"

"Like . . . a burnt offering. You know the Herdmans."

Well, they did burn things, but they hadn't burned this yet. It was a ham—and right away I knew where it came from. My father was on the church charitable works committee—they give away food baskets at Christmas, and this was the Herdman's food-basket ham. It still had the ribbon around it, saying Merry Christmas.

"I'll bet they stole that!" Alice said.

"They did not. It came from their food basket, and if they want to give away their own ham I guess they can do it." But even if the Herdmans didn't *like* ham (that was Alice's next idea) they had never before in their lives given anything away except lumps on the head. So you had to be impressed.

Leroy dropped the ham in front of the manger. It looked funny to see a ham there instead of the fancy bath-salts jars we always used for the myrrh and the frankincense. And then they went and sat down in the only space that was left.

While we sang "What Child Is This?" the Wise Men were supposed to confer among themselves and then leave by a different door, so everyone would understand that they were going home another way. But the Herdmans forgot, or didn't want to, or something, because they didn't confer and they didn't leave either. They just sat there, and there wasn't anything anyone could do about it.

"They're ruining the whole thing!" Alice whispered, but they weren't at all. As a matter of fact, it made perfect sense for the Wise Men to sit down and rest, and I said so.

"They're supposed to have come a long way. You wouldn't expect them just to show up, hand over the ham, and leave!"

As for ruining the whole thing, it seemed to me that the Herdmans had improved the pageant a lot, just by doing what came naturally—like burping the baby, for instance, or thinking a ham would make a better present than a lot of perfumed oil.

Usually, by the time we got to "Silent Night,"

which was always the last carol, I was fed up with the whole thing and couldn't wait for it to be over. But I didn't feel that way this time. I almost wished for the pageant to go on, with the Herdmans in charge, to see what else they would do that was different.

Maybe the Wise Men would tell Mary about their problem with Herod, and she would tell them to go back and lie their heads off. Or Joseph might go with them and get rid of Herod once and for all. Or Joseph and Mary might ask the Wise Men to take the Christ Child with them, figuring that no one would think to look there.

I was so busy planning new ways to save the baby Jesus that I missed the beginning of "Silent Night," but it was all right because everyone sang "Silent Night," including the audience. We sang all the verses too, and when we got to "Son of God, Love's pure light" I happened to look at Imogene and I almost dropped my hymn book on a baby angel.

Everyone had been waiting all this time for the Herdmans to do something absolutely unexpected. And sure enough, that was what happened.

Imogene Herdman was crying.

In the candlelight her face was all shiny with tears and she didn't even bother to wipe them away. She just sat there—awful old Imogene—in her crookedy veil, crying and crying and crying.

Well. It *was* the best Christmas pageant we ever had.

Everybody said so, but nobody seemed to know why. When it was over people stood around the lobby of the church talking about what was different this year. There was something special, everyone said—they couldn't put their finger on what.

Mrs. Wendleken said, "Well, Mary the mother of Jesus had a black eye; that was something special. But only what you might expect," she added.

She meant that it was the most natural thing in the world for a Herdman to have a black eye. But actually nobody hit Imogene and she didn't hit anyone else. Her eye wasn't really black either, just all puffy and swollen. She had walked into the corner of the choir-robe cabinet, in a kind of daze—as if she had just caught onto the idea of God, and the wonder of Christmas.

And this was the funny thing about it all. For years, I'd thought about the wonder of Christmas, and the mystery of Jesus' birth, and never really understood it. But now, because of the Herdmans, it didn't seem so mysterious after all.

When Imogene had asked me what the pageant was about, I told her it was about Jesus, but that was just part of it. It was about a new baby, and his mother and father who were in a lot of trouble—no money, no place to go, no doctor, nobody they knew. And then, arriving from the East (like my uncle from New Jersey) some rich friends.

But Imogene, I guess, didn't see it that way. Christmas just came over her all at once, like a case of chills and fever. And so she was crying, and walking into the furniture.

Afterward there were candy canes and little tiny Testaments for everyone, and a poinsettia plant for my mother from the whole Sunday school. We put the costumes away and folded up the collapsible manger, and just before we left, my father snuffed out the last of the tall white candles.

"I guess that's everything," he said as we stood at the back of the church. "All over now. It was quite a pageant." Then he looked at my mother.

"What's that you've got?"

"It's the ham," she said. "They wouldn't take it back. They wouldn't take any candy either, or any of the little Bibles. But Imogene did ask me for a set of the Bible-story pictures, and she took out the Mary picture and said it was exactly right, whatever that means."

I think it meant that no matter how she herself was, Imogene liked the idea of the Mary in the picture—all pink and white and pure-looking, as if she never washed the dishes or cooked supper or did anything at all except have Jesus on Christmas Eve.

But as far as I'm concerned, Mary is always going to look a lot like Imogene Herdman—sort of nervous and bewildered, but ready to clobber anyone who laid a hand on her baby. And the Wise Men are always going to be Leroy and his brothers, bearing ham.

When we came out of the church that night it was cold and clear, with crunchy snow underfoot and bright, bright stars overhead. And I thought about the Angel of the Lord—Gladys, with her skinny legs and her dirty sneakers sticking out from under her robe, yelling at all of us, everywhere:

"Hey! Unto you a child is born!"

Barbara Robinson was born in Portsmouth, Ohio, but now makes her home in Berwyn, Pennsylvania. The recipient of a B.A. degree from Allegheny College, Ms. Robinson has written several books for children, including, most recently, MY BROTHER LOUIS MEASURES WORMS: AND OTHER LOUIS STORIES; *and* TEMPORARY TIMES, TEMPORARY PLACES, *which was an ALA Notable Book and a* School Library Journal Best Book, *both in 1982.* THE BEST CHRISTMAS PAGEANT EVER *was among the ALA Notable Children's Books of 1971–75, and was produced as an ABC television film in 1983. Ms. Robinson has also published numerous short stories in well-known magazines.*

She and her husband have two daughters, Carolyn and Marjorie.